Grumpy Bear

written by Pam Holden
illustrated by Kelvin Hawley

Grumpy Bear wanted to have a long sleep
The other animals made too much noise.
He couldn't get to sleep.

One night he made a trap to catch
the animals.
He put sticks and leaves over the trap.

The next day Goat fell down into the trap.
He called out for someone to help him.
Grumpy Bear came to take him far away.

Goat said, "Take me anywhere, but please don't put me up on the mountain."
Grumpy Bear didn't know that goats like mountains.
So he put Goat way up on the mountain.
Goat was happy there.

The next day, Monkey fell into Grumpy Bear's trap.
He called out for help.
Grumpy Bear came to take him far away.

Monkey said, "Take me far away, but please don't put me in the forest."
Grumpy Bear said, "I will put you in the forest."
Monkey was happy there because monkeys like forests.

Soon Duck fell down into Grumpy Bear's trap.
He called out for help. "Quack! Quack!"
Grumpy Bear came to take him away.
Duck said, "Take me anywhere, but please don't put me in the pond."

Grumpy Bear said, "I will put you in the pond."
Duck was happy there with his friends.
Ducks like ponds.

Next Pig fell into Grumpy Bear's trap.
He called out for someone to help him.
Grumpy Bear came to take him away.

Pig said, "Please don't put me in the mud."
But Grumpy Bear said, "I will put you in the mud."
He didn't know that pigs like mud.
Pig was very happy there.

Grumpy Bear went back to his cave to sleep all winter.
The animals came back to play.
They were all happy and noisy!